Diego Saves the Sloth!

by Alexis Romay

illustrated by Art Mawhinney

Simon Spotlight/Nick Jr.

New York   London   Toronto   Sydney

visit us at www.abdopublishing.com

Reinforced library bound edition published in 2009 by Spotlight, a division of ABDO Publishing Group, 8000 West 78th Street, Edina, Minnesota 55439. Published by agreement with Simon Spotlight, an imprint of Simon & Schuster Children's Publishing Division.

SIMON SPOTLIGHT

An imprint of Simon & Schuster Children's Publishing Division
1230 Avenue of the Americas, New York, NY 10020

Library of Congress Cataloging-in-Publication Data

This title was previously cataloged with the following information:
Romay, Alexis.
  Diego saves the sloth! / by Alexis Romay ; illustrated by Art Mawhinney.
    p. cm. -- (Go, Diego, Go!; #4)
  "Based on the TV series Go, Diego, go! as seen on Nick Jr."
  Summary: Diego saves Sammy the Sloth who is stranded on a tree branch.
  [1. Sloths--Juvenile fiction. 2. Rescues--Juvenile fiction. 3. Adventures--Juvenile Fiction.] I. Mawhinney, Art, ill. II. Go, Diego, Go! (Television program). III. Title. IV. Series.
  [E]--dc22   2007299566

ISBN-13: 978-1-59961-430-4 (reinforced library bound edition)
ISBN-10: 1-59961-430-8 (reinforced library bound edition)

All Spotlight books have reinforced library binding and are manufactured in the United States of America.

¡Hola! Soy Diego. I'm an Animal Rescuer. It's a very windy day, so I'm making sure all of the animals are getting back to their homes safely! Will you help?

Click the Camera can help us find all of our animal friends to make sure that they're safe! Do you see any animals in trouble?

Oh, no! Sammy the Sloth is in trouble! If the winds break his branch, he could fall and get hurt.

Alicia used the computer to look up information that we need to know about sloths so we can save Sammy! Sloths live in trees and move very slowly.

Sloths are most active at night and sleep all day. Look! Sammy is sound asleep! He doesn't even know that there's a big windstorm blowing!

We have to save Sammy!

¡Al rescate! To the rescue! Let's use our zip cord to get to Sammy.
Hang on tight! The wind is strong!

We'll need to fly over the rainforest to get to Sammy on the other side. Rescue Pack can turn into anything we need.

What vehicle would work best to fly in the wind and go over the rainforest? *¡Sí!* A hang glider! To activate Rescue Pack, say *"¡Actívate!"*

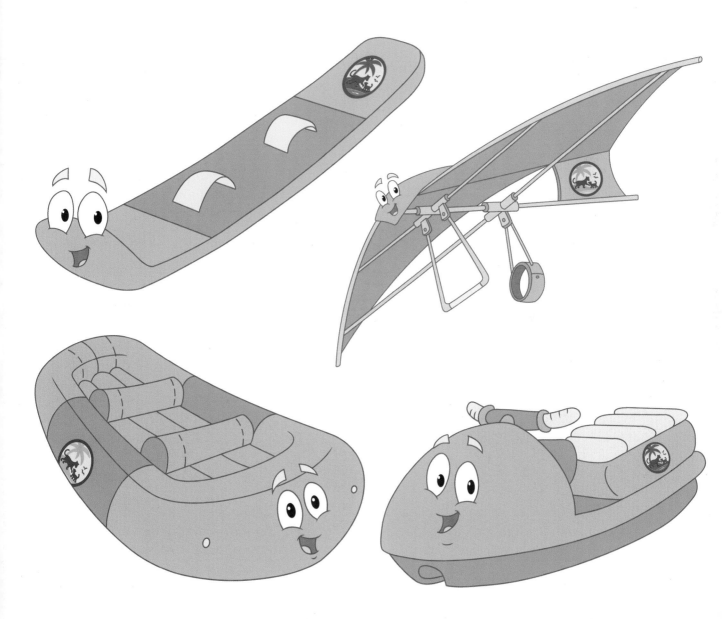

To get above the woods, we need to fly high. To go up, up, and away, we need to say *"¡Arriba!"*

Hang on, Sammy! Here we come!

We need to wake up Sammy and help him move to a stronger branch—and quick! Help me call Sammy's name to wake him up!

"Sammy, wake up! *¡Despierta!*"

Oh, no! Sammy didn't hear us! The wind is too loud!
Look! Now those silly Bobo Brothers are playing on Sammy's branch!
Between them and the wind, that branch is going to break!

We need to stop the Bobo Brothers. To stop them, say "Freeze, Bobos!"

Thanks for helping me stop the Bobo Brothers. But look! The wind made Sammy's branch break! *¡Rápido!* We need to get to Sammy quickly!

We saved Sammy the Sloth! *¡Excelente!*
Let's help him find a nice, safe tree where he'll be able to sleep safely.

¡Misión cumplida! Rescue complete! Thanks for helping me save Sammy! *¡Gracias!*

Did you know?

Home sweet home

Sloths live on trees. They rarely go down to the ground.

Sloths are nocturnal, which means that they are most active at night and sleep all day. A sloth can sleep for up to fifteen hours per day!

Upside down

Sloths eat and sleep while hanging upside down! They don't even get dizzy!

In the water

In spite of the fact that they are very slow, sloths are very good swimmers!

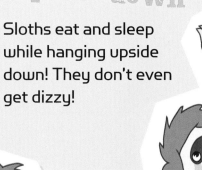